Library of Congress Cataloging-in-Publication Data
Big Pig and Little Pig/Age of Learning, Inc.
Summary: In this Word Family Beginning Reader, a little pig
finds a fig and shares it with a big pig.

ISBN: 9781621160113
Library of Congress Control Number: 2012912299

21 20 19 18 17 16 15 14 13 12   1 2 3 4 5
Printed in the U.S.A., on 10% recycled paper. ♻
First printing, September 2012

Big Pig and Little Pig

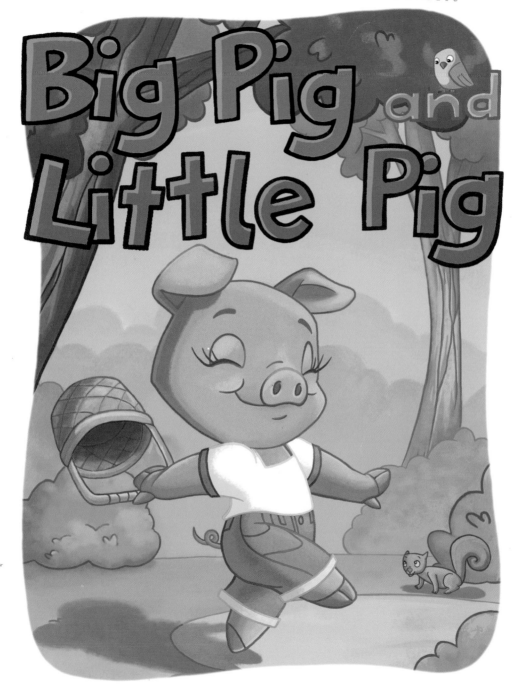

Age of Learning, Inc., Glendale, California
This book is also available at **ABCmouse.com**, the award-winning early learning online curriculum.
Find free apps at **ABCmouse.com/apps**.

A little pig found
a fig.

Then she did a
little jig.

The little pig
liked to dig.
She dug a hole
to hide the fig.

A big pig saw
the little pig. He
saw her dig and
hide the fig.

The big pig said to the little pig, "I would like to eat a fig! Will you dig and find the fig?"

"Yes, I will!" said
the little pig.

Then the little pig did dig. She found the fig for the big pig.

He took a bite
out of the fig.

He gave the rest
to the little pig.

"Yum! Yum! Yum!"
said the little pig.

And then she did
a little jig!

The End